LITTLE
LAMB

For Regan

LITTLE LAMB

Piers Harper

Cartwheel
B·O·O·K·S®

SCHOLASTIC INC.

New York   Toronto   London   Auckland   Sydney   Mexico City   New Delhi   Hong Kong   Buenos Aires

Little Lamb and her mother lived in a green, green field with many other lambs and their mothers.

The lambs loved to play hide-and-seek.
"Come and find me!" called Little Lamb,
and she skipped away to find
a place to hide.

Little Lamb ran into the bushes.
"They won't find me in here!"
she giggled to herself.
But behind the bushes she saw
another green, green field,
and in that green, green field
there was an animal she had
never seen before.

"BAA!" said Little Lamb. "I am looking for a good place to hide. Can you help me?"

"MOO!" said a cow. "This meadow is filled with big cows like me. You might get bumped around. Go over to the barn. That's a good place for a little lamb to hide."

So Little Lamb skipped over to the barn
and saw animals with squiggly tails eating
their lunch.

"BAA!" said Little Lamb.
"I am looking for a good place to hide.
Can you help me?"

"OINK, OINK!" said the pigs. "You don't want to hide here. You will get dirty. Go down to the pond. That's a good place for a little lamb to hide."

So Little Lamb hurried down to the pond.

"BAA!" said Little Lamb. "I'm looking for a good place to hide. Can you help me?"

"QUACK, QUACK!" said the duck. "You don't want to hide in this pond. You can't swim. Go back to your mother. That's the best place for a little lamb like you."

Little Lamb forgot all about the game
of hide-and-seek and went to find her mother.

"Where is she?" said Little Lamb,
and she started to cry.

In the distance she heard a dog barking,
"WOOF, WOOF!"

"I found you!" said a friendly voice. Little Lamb looked up.
It was Piper, the sheepdog.

"Well, Little Lamb, what a good hiding place this is!
Your friends have been looking for you everywhere,
and your mother is worried. Let's go home."

Little Lamb followed Piper across the farmyard
to the green, green field she knew.

"I am glad you are home!" said her mother.
Little Lamb ran to her side.

Little Lamb nuzzled her mother.
The next time she played hide-and-seek,
she wouldn't stray so far.
"BAA! I love you!" said Little Lamb.
"BAA! I love you, too," said her mother.

The End